THE ZACK FILES™

Yikes! Grandma's a Teenager

By Dan Greenburg

Illustrated by Jack E. Davis

GROSSET & DUNLAP • NEW YORK

I'd like to thank my editor
Jane O'Connor who makes the process
of writing and revising so much fun,
and without whom
these books would not exist.

I also want to thank Catherine Daly,
Laura Driscoll, and Emily Neye
for their terrific ideas.

Text copyright © 1999 by Dan Greenburg. Illustrations copyright © 1999 by Jack E. Davis. All rights reserved. Published by Grosset & Dunlap, a division of Penguin Putnam Books for Young Readers, New York. GROSSET & DUNLAP and THE ZACK FILES are trademarks of Penguin Putnam Inc. Published simultaneously in Canada. Printed in the U.S.A.

Library of Congress Cataloging-in-Publication Data.

Greenburg, Dan.
    Yikes! Grandma's a teenager / by Dan Greenburg ; illustrated by Jack E. Davis.
    p. cm. -- (The Zack files ; 17)
    Summary: A strange trip through a metal detector causes Zack's eighty-eight year old Grandma Leah to get younger and younger.
    [1. Grandmothers--Fiction. 2. Supernatural--Fiction.] I. Davis, Jack E., ill. II. Title.

PZ7.G8278 Yi 1999
[Fic]--dc21   99-035534

ISBN 0-448-41999-8   G H I J

Chapter 1

Why is it everybody wants to be some age they aren't? Every kid I know wants to be older. Every grown-up I know wants to be younger. That kills me, boy. Why would anybody want to be younger? I mean, I've *been* younger, and it's not so great. And the story I'm about to tell you proves what I'm saying.

Oh, I should say who I am and stuff. My name is Zack. I'm ten and a half, going on eleven. I go to the Horace Hyde–White School for Boys in New York City. My parents are divorced, and I spend half my time with each of them.

It's always when I'm with Dad that something weird happens. Like the time I opened his refrigerator and found a turnip that looked and sang just like Elvis Presley. Or the time Dad took me to this Chinese restaurant and all the fortunes in the fortune cookies started coming true. Or the time Dad and I found a UFO in the park and saved a space creature's life.

Or like this time I'm going to tell you about with my Grandma Leah.

Grandma Leah is my dad's mom. She's eighty-eight years old. She lives in Chicago, where my dad grew up. When my grandma was a girl in Poland, she was this really terrific dancer. Then she came to New York. She got a job dancing at Radio City Music Hall as a Rockette.

The Rockettes are a bunch of ladies who

dance in a long line, arm in arm. They kick their legs way up high. They do it at exactly the same time, the way guys in the Army march. I don't mean guys in the Army dance in a long line, kicking their legs up, but you get the idea.

Anyway, Radio City Music Hall was having this big party, a Rockettes Reunion. They found out my grandma was the oldest living Rockette. They asked her to come to New York to be part of the celebration. She would stay for a week. While she was in New York, we'd get to celebrate her eighty-ninth birthday. And she'd come to school for Grandparents Day.

Dad and I went out to the airport to meet Grandma Leah and bring her back to Dad's apartment. Her plane landed. All the people arrived. But no Grandma Leah. Dad was getting worried. Then we heard this *beep-beep*, and there she was. On a little electric cart, driven by a guy in a blue uniform. Grandma Leah looked confused and a little dizzy.

"Grandma!" I said. "Where were you?"

"Mom, we were so worried!" said Dad. "What happened to you?"

"I got lost," she said. "I was looking for the baggage claim. And I somehow ended up where you go to get on other airplanes."

"What happened then?" asked my dad, helping Grandma Leah off the electric cart.

"I was so confused, I went through the metal detector *backwards*. It made loud noises. Sparks shot out. It caused quite a fuss, I tell you. They said it never happened before. I have no idea what I did. I do hope I didn't break their machine."

"Oh, Mom, I doubt that you broke their machine," said Dad. He hugged her again. We picked up Grandma's bags and left.

When we got to Dad's apartment, Grandma Leah unpacked and showed us her old photo album. She had brought it for the Rockettes reunion. There were pictures of Grandma's husband, Grandpa Sam. There were pictures of Great-Grandpa Maurice when he was a person, before he died and came back as a cat. There were pictures of Grandma in some of her Rockettes outfits. She looked so beautiful and happy. I wish I'd known her when she was that young.

She also showed us her Rockettes bracelet. Grandma jangled her wrist in front of me. "I bet I haven't worn this in over fifty years."

The bracelet was copper, with several crystals set into it. One crystal was a milky color; another was green and seemed to glow. One was purple and was kind of tingly to the touch. On the bracelet, in tiny script, was written, "Radio City: Experience the Magic."

"I found it when I was going through all my old stuff," said Grandma Leah. "I thought I'd wear it to the party."

Then Grandma yawned. "You know, I'm still feeling a little woozy. I think I will have some hot tea and then go straight to bed."

And that is just what she did.

"Boy," I said, "that thing at the airport seems to have really upset her. I hope she'll be all right in the morning."

"I bet she'll be fine," Dad said. "All she needs is a good night's sleep."

And Dad was sure right about that. In the morning, Grandma Leah woke up feeling like her old self.

"How do you feel, Mom?" asked my dad.

"I feel like my old self," said my grandma. "In fact, I feel *better* than my old self."

"Wonderful," said my dad. "You know, you do look great, Mom. In fact, you look younger than you have in years."

I took a closer look at Grandma. She did look wonderful. And she did look younger. Lots younger.

"I feel like a woman of seventy," she said.

Dad studied her closely.

"You know," he said, "you even *look* like a woman of seventy. How could that be?"

Grandma Leah walked to the full-length mirror on the bathroom door. She studied her reflection. She was standing up straighter. She had fewer wrinkles on her face. She was wearing a big smile.

"It must be the mattress on the bed," she said. "I had a great night's sleep. And I feel like I'm bursting with energy."

Grandma Leah wasn't kidding. She spent the whole time I was at school cleaning the apartment. She washed all the windows. She wanted to paint all the walls and ceilings, but Dad stopped her.

The next morning, Grandma Leah woke

up feeling even better than she had the day before. And she looked even younger. By dinnertime, a stranger probably would have guessed she was no more than fifty.

"Look at you, Mom!" said Dad as he passed her the chicken. "You look fabulous!"

"Holy guacamole, Grandma!" I said. There were hardly any wrinkles in her face or neck. And her hair was way more brown than gray. "You look almost the same age as Dad!" I said.

"Really?" said Grandma Leah. She rushed from the table to the bathroom mirror. I'd never seen her move so fast. "Oh, no!" she cried. "This is terrible!"

"Huh?" said Dad.

"What?" I said.

"This is terrible!" said Grandma Leah.

"Terrible?" I repeated. "How could it be terrible?"

"It is not natural," she said, "for a woman of eighty-eight—almost eighty-nine —to look this young. It's wrong. It is against the laws of nature."

"Mom," said my dad, "anybody in the world would *kill* to suddenly look years younger."

"Well, I am not anybody in the world," said my grandma. "For me to look so young is…is frightening."

"Frightening?" I said.

"Yes," said Grandma Leah. "We must do something to make me look old again."

"Like what?" I asked.

"Maybe I should try to stay up all night tonight," said Grandma Leah.

Dad and I looked at each other. We both thought my grandma was being a little cuckoo. But we do love her. And we didn't want her to be so upset.

"OK, Mom," said my dad. "Whatever you say."

"Tomorrow is Sunday," said Grandma Leah. "The day of the rehearsal for the Rockettes reunion. Remember?" She pointed to the Rockettes bracelet she had on. "I have to look my best. I mean, I have to look *old*."

"OK," said Dad. "I'll get some coffee brewing. Then let's look in the paper and see what late night movies are on TV. I bet if you stay up all night, you'll have terrible bags under your eyes and look really awful by tomorrow."

"You are a wonderful son," said Grandma Leah.

Dad and I looked at each other again. Something weird was definitely going on. But what?

Chapter 2

Early Sunday morning I was awakened by a scream. I jumped out of bed. I dashed out of my bedroom.

Standing in front of the full-length mirror on the bathroom door was Grandma Leah. Except it wasn't Grandma Leah. It was a teenaged version of Grandma Leah. The only way I knew it was Grandma was that she was wearing Grandma's fuzzy pink slippers, her fluffy pink robe, and her Rockettes bracelet.

"This is…like…*amazing*," she said.

"Grandma?"

"This is…like…totally *awesome*," she said.

She couldn't stop looking at herself in the mirror.

"Grandma, is that really you?" I asked. I sounded like Little Red Riding Hood.

"Of course, dear," she said. She was still staring into the mirror. "But this is so…*cool*."

"Uh…yeah" was all I could think of to say.

"And look at this," she said. She pointed to her chin. "Zits."

I looked. She was right. She had two big pimples on her chin.

Just then, my dad walked into the room. He wasn't wearing his glasses. He was rubbing his eyes from sleep.

"I thought I heard somebody scream," he said. "But maybe I dreamed it. Did somebody scream?"

Then he saw Grandma Leah. He screamed.

"Wh-who are you?" he demanded. I think he knew, though. Which is why he screamed.

"Who *am* I?" Grandma repeated. "*Duh*. Like, hel-*lo*-o. I'm your mother. Who else would I be?"

"But you look like...a teenager."

"Yeah," she giggled. She turned to face him. "Isn't it awesome?"

My dad looked like he was going to pass out or something. He leaned against a wall to keep his balance.

"How did this happen?" he whispered.

Grandma Leah shrugged.

"I wake up," she said, "and I'm like, 'What is *up* with me?' I mean, I felt so,

like, *weird*. You know? Then I pass by the bathroom mirror, and *Whoa*! So then Zack comes in, and he goes, 'Grandma, is that really you?'"

She giggled again.

"Grandma," I said, "I don't get it. Last night you were so upset about getting younger. But being a teenager doesn't seem to bother you at all. How come?"

"It's because last night she still had the good judgment of an adult," Dad whispered. "But now she's a crazy teenager."

"Zack, listen," she said, "I grew up in, like, Poland, OK? I mean, I was a teenager in *Poland*. How boring is *that*? Now I get to be a teenager in *America*. In *New York*, right?"

"Uh...yeah," I said. "I sort of see your point. Sort of."

Grandma went into her room and closed the door.

I turned to see how Dad was doing. He wasn't looking so good.

"Well," I said, "at least she seems happy about it."

"How could my mother have become a teenager?" said my dad. "I don't understand." He kept shaking his head.

Grandma Leah came out of her room. She was completely dressed. She looked weird, though. A teenager in old-lady clothes. She walked to the front door.

"Where are you going?" Dad asked.

"Out," said Grandma.

"Out where?"

"What are you, my father?" she asked.

"No," said Dad, "your son. I just want to know where you're going."

"Shopping," said Grandma. "I have to, like, buy some stuff. You know?"

"What kind of stuff are you going to buy?" Dad asked.

"*Stuff*," said Grandma. "A miniskirt. Some platform shoes. Some cool lipstick. You know? Maybe I can even find a place that does body piercing. I'm thinking of getting, like, a ring in my eyebrow."

"What if I don't think that's such a good idea?" Dad asked.

Grandma put her hands on her hips. She looked annoyed.

"What if you don't think that's such a good *idea*?" Grandma repeated. "Hel-*lo*-o. I'm your *mother*, OK?"

"Today is the Rockettes rehearsal at Radio City Music Hall," Dad said. "At two o'clock."

"So?" said Grandma Leah.

"So," said Dad, "try to be back here by one. And tonight you've got that interview with *Entertainment Weekly* magazine."

Grandma kissed us both good-bye and left.

"Oh, boy," said Dad.

"What?"

"I can't wait for that rehearsal," said Dad. "I can't wait to see what they think of the oldest living Rockette."

Chapter 3

Radio City Music Hall is on Sixth Avenue, at Rockefeller Center. It's one of the biggest theaters in the world. They have this humongous organ. Every Christmas they have this huge Christmas show. The Rockettes dance there and stuff. Thousands of people come to see them.

At two in the afternoon on a day when they don't have a show, Radio City Music Hall is deserted. A guard at the door looked us over.

"May I help you?" the guard asked. He didn't look like he wanted to, though.

"We're here for the rehearsal," said my dad.

"Who are you?" said the guard.

"My mother is the oldest living Rockette," said Dad. He pointed to me. "And this is her grandson."

The guard nodded. Then he looked at my grandma. She was wearing her new clothes. A black miniskirt. Big platform shoes. Black lipstick.

"Who are you, the granddaughter?" he asked.

"No," said Grandma, "I'm—"

"That's exactly who she is," said my dad. "The granddaughter. Can we go in?"

"And where's the old lady?" asked the guard.

"She's...here," said my dad.

"You mean she's already in the theater?"

Dad didn't say yes and he didn't say no.

"She's right here at Radio City Music Hall," said Dad. "So can we go in?"

"I guess so," said the guard.

He opened the door to the theater. We went in.

It was even bigger than I remembered. There were about a million seats. Balconies went up to the ceiling. The ceiling was so high, you could jump off the top balcony in a parachute. You'd probably kill yourself, though, because it wouldn't open in time.

Up on stage were a bunch of people. Some Rockettes in street clothes. Some other people. A man was standing in front of the stage. He wore a baseball cap and was holding a clipboard. I figured he was the director. When he saw us, he walked over.

"Are you in the show?" he asked.

"Yes," said my grandma.

"Good," said the director. "We're almost ready to start." He looked at his clipboard. "Name?"

"I'm Grandma Leah," said my grandma. "I'm, like, the oldest living Rockette?"

The director looked up.

"Who are you, hon, her granddaughter?" he asked.

"No, dude," said Grandma, "I'm *her*. Grandma Leah. Hel-*lo*-o. Read my lips."

The director looked at Dad.

"Will Grandma Leah be arriving soon?" he asked. "Because we really do have to get started here."

"She is telling the truth," said my dad. "She really is my mother. She's been getting younger and younger every day. When she arrived in New York, she looked eighty-eight. The next day she looked seventy. The next day she looked *my* age…"

"And then today she woke up looking like this," I said. "We're not sure why this is happening, sir."

The director looked at me. Then at Dad. Then at Grandma Leah. Then at me.

"I suppose you people think this is a big yuck," he said. "Well, we're very busy here. We don't have time for big yucks. I'd like you to leave now. Either come back with Grandma Leah or don't come back at all."

It was pretty obvious the reporter from *Entertainment Weekly* wasn't going to believe teenaged Grandma Leah was the oldest living Rockette. But she really wanted to do the interview. So Dad called the magazine and said Grandma had this really bad cold, and maybe they could do the interview on the phone. The reporter said fine.

Grandma did the interview from the phone in Dad's study. I listened in on the phone in the kitchen.

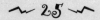

25

"So," said the reporter, "you're the oldest living Rockette. Exactly how old *are* you, ma'am?"

"I'm, you know, eighty-eight," said Grandma Leah. "I'll be eighty-nine, on, like, Tuesday."

"Astounding," said the reporter. "You sound so much younger. If I didn't know better, I'd say you were...oh, at least ten years younger than that."

"Yeah, well," said Grandma Leah, "people do say I sound about seventy-eight."

"So tell me. What was it like at Radio City Music Hall?" said the reporter.

"Well," said Grandma Leah, "I remember that it was so *not* fun. This director goes, 'Are you in the show?' And I'm, like, 'Yes.' So he goes, 'Good, we're almost ready to start.' And he's, like, 'Name?' So I go, 'I'm Grandma Leah. I'm, like, the oldest living Rockette?' So—"

"Wait a minute," said the reporter. "How long ago was this?"

"Like about two o'clock?" said Grandma Leah.

"Two o'clock...*today*," said the reporter.

"Well, *duh*," said Grandma Leah.

"I was hoping for a memory that was more than three hours old," said the reporter.

Chapter 4

The next day was Monday. Grandparents Day.

Dad and I got up early. We were kind of nervous to see what age Grandma was going to be when she woke up. We knew she was awake. We could hear her banging around in her room. Then her door opened, and Grandma walked into the living room.

"Hey, what time is breakfast?" she asked. "I'm, like, starving to death here.

Could I have, like, three chocolate-covered doughnuts and a Coke?"

"Grandma," I said, "you're still a teenager."

"Well, *duh*," said my grandma.

"I mean, I thought you might have gotten even younger," I explained.

"Well, I didn't," said my grandma.

"We don't have chocolate-covered doughnuts and a Coke," said my dad.

"OK," said my grandma. "I'll take, like, Pop Tarts and a Dr. Pepper."

"That's not a healthy breakfast," said Dad.

"Who cares?" said Grandma Leah.

"I do," said Dad. "You're a growing girl."

"I'm eighty-eight and I'm growing *younger*, not older," said Grandma Leah.

"She does have a point there," I said.

Dad sighed and shook his head.

"Tell me, Mom," he said, "is *that* what you're planning to wear to Grandparents Day?"

"What's wrong with this?" said Grandma Leah, looking down at her leopard-print miniskirt.

"Well, I just wondered if you had anything else."

"I could change to my *leather* miniskirt," said Grandma. "And, like, this really cool motorcycle jacket I bought."

"Never mind," said Dad. "What you're wearing is fine."

When we got to my school, a lot of the grandparents were already in my homeroom talking to Mrs. Coleman-Levin. Vernon Manteuffel's were there, and so were Spencer Sharp's. Both Vernon and Spencer had normal-looking grandparents. Not me.

Mrs. Coleman-Levin is not only our homeroom teacher. She is also our science teacher. She had set up a table with food for our guests. There was coffee and tea. There were little tiny sandwiches. There were also cookies and cake and stuff.

Andrew Clancy came over to say hello. He's this guy in my class who's always trying to top me.

"This is my friend Andrew," I said to Dad and Grandma. "Andrew, this is my dad and my Grandma Leah."

Andrew shook hands with Dad, then with Grandma Leah.

"Your grandma looks awful young," said Andrew.

I nodded like it was no big deal.

"Well, my grandparents are even younger than yours," Andrew announced.

"Are they here today?" Dad asked.

"Oh, no," said Andrew. "They couldn't

come. They're playing in a championship Little League game. Grandma's pitching."

Just then Mrs. Coleman-Levin came over to say hello.

"Mrs. Coleman-Levin," I said, "this is my dad and my Grandma Leah."

"Pleased to meet you," she said.

Mrs. Coleman-Levin is pretty cool for an adult. You could tell she was dying of curiosity, though.

"You look remarkably...youthful for your age," said Mrs. Coleman-Levin to my grandma.

"Thanks," said my grandma. "You know, I was, like, a Rockette about sixty years ago."

Mrs. Coleman-Levin smiled and nodded. Then she took me aside. "Zack, might I be witnessing an incredible case of reverse-aging?" she asked.

"Yes, ma'am," I said.

"I thought so," said Mrs. Coleman-Levin. She went back to talk more with Grandma Leah. I saw Grandma showing off her Rockettes bracelet.

"Those are very unusual crystals in that bracelet," said Mrs. Coleman-Levin. "The greenish one in particular. It has a strong electromagnetic field. Natives of Pongo-Pongo believe such crystals have very unusual properties."

Mrs. Coleman-Levin knows all about the weird stuff that has happened to me. Like the time Spencer and I traveled out of our bodies and couldn't get back in again. Or the time I drank disappearing ink and became invisible. So Grandma's appearance did not freak her out.

All the grandparents, however, thought Grandma Leah was my older sister. We tried to explain to them, but they just didn't get it. After a while, we gave up trying.

When everybody arrived, Mrs. Coleman-Levin made a short speech. She welcomed all the grandparents. She asked them to tell about their childhoods. Everybody had pretty interesting stories to tell. I couldn't wait for my grandma to tell about her childhood in Poland. But when I looked over at her, I realized she wasn't even paying attention. She was listening to music on headphones.

"Pssst, Grandma," I whispered.

She didn't hear me. I pulled the headphones away from her ears.

"Grandma, what are you doing?" I whispered.

"Listening to hip-hop," she answered. "This CD is awesome."

"Grandma," I said, "you're embarrassing me."

She shrugged. She put the headphones back on her ears.

I stared at Grandma. This was really beyond weird. This was rude. I mean, I've known my grandma my whole life. What was happening to her? She was acting so immature. I mean, there she was with her black lipstick. And her leopard-print miniskirt. And her black leather motorcycle jacket with all the zippers. The only thing that made me know it was her was the Rockettes bracelet on her wrist.

And then I realized something. Grandma's miniskirt no longer fit her. Neither did her motorcycle jacket. They were both way too big. But this morning, they had fit. And her skin had somehow cleared up. Her zits were gone.

I had an awful feeling that I knew what was going on. Grandma Leah was starting to get younger again, right before my very eyes!

I pulled the headphones away from her ears.

"Grandma," I whispered, "something's

happening to you. I think you're growing younger again."

"I am?" she said. She looked confused.

"Yes," I whispered.

She thought a moment. She frowned.

"Something's wrong with this music, too," she said. Her voice sounded higher than before. She took off her headphones.

"This music is so...stupid," she said.

She got up out of her seat. She wandered over to the food table. And this was while Vernon's grandma was telling a funny story about her first time on a plane. I didn't think Grandma Leah was being too polite. I went over to Dad.

"I'm worried about Grandma," I whispered. "I think she's started getting younger again."

I pointed to Grandma at the food table.

"Her clothes don't seem to fit anymore," he said.

"She's getting smaller," I explained.

Grandma Leah put a bunch of sandwiches and other food on a paper plate and went back to her seat. On the way back, she tripped over one of the kids' backpacks. She didn't fall, but she looked embarrassed.

Steven laughed at her, which was a big mistake. Because Grandma Leah took a sandwich and threw it at him. Steven was shocked. Then he threw the sandwich back at her.

"Food fight!" yelled Vernon. He ran to the table to get food to throw. In less than a second, a major food fight was in progress.

"Vernon! Steven! Andrew! Grandma Leah!" yelled Mrs. Coleman-Levin. "You stop that this instant!"

Everybody froze. Grandma Leah, too. They looked pretty scared. Mrs. Coleman-

Levin can yell really loudly when she wants to.

"Do you want me to send all of you down to the principal's office?" shouted Mrs. Coleman-Levin. "Is that what you want me to do?"

The guys and Grandma Leah all shook their heads.

"I'm ashamed of all of you," said Mrs. Coleman-Levin. "Especially in front of our guests. I'm ashamed of the boys, but they're only ten. You, Grandma Leah, should know better, though. You're an adult."

"Am not," said Grandma Leah.

"Are too," said Mrs. Coleman-Levin.

"Am not," said Grandma Leah.

So Mrs. Coleman-Levin sent my grandma to the principal's office.

Chapter 5

After we left school, we got into a cab.

"I just don't know what to do with you, Mom," said Dad. "Even if you're getting younger and younger, it's not like you to act so...naughty."

"Steven started it," said Grandma Leah.

"But, Mom, you threw the sandwich at him first," said Dad.

"Yeah, but he laughed at me," said Grandma Leah.

Dad just rolled his eyes.

We got out of the cab at a girls' clothing store. Dad wanted to buy stuff that fit my grandma. Her miniskirt and motorcycle jacket were so big she was swimming in them.

"May I help you?" said a saleswoman. She was staring at Grandma in a disapproving way.

"Yes," said my dad. "We need to buy a dress or something to replace what she's wearing."

"You can say *that* again," said the saleswoman.

"Excuse me?" said Dad.

"I'd never let any eight-year-old daughter of *mine* dress like that," said the saleswoman.

"Neither would I," said Dad. "But she was a teenager only this morning. And by the way, she's not my daughter. She's my mother."

"Whatever you say," said the sales-woman.

She went to get some dresses to show us.

"I'm sorry I've been a brat," said Grandma Leah. "I'm sorry if I embarrassed you. I really am. I mean it." She was getting all teary-eyed.

Dad sighed.

"That's all right, dear," he said. "You're just going through a difficult phase."

"I know it," said my grandma.

"It's not your fault, Grandma," I said.

"I know it," she said. "Plus which, Steven *did* start it."

"Here's what worries me," I said. "Grandma's getting younger and younger, OK? Pretty soon she'll be about five. And pretty soon after that, she'll become a baby. Then an embryo. And then, unless we do something fast, pretty soon she'll disappear altogether."

Grandma Leah burst into tears.

"Oh, no!" she wailed. "Oh, no-o-o-o-o-o!"

"And if Grandma Leah disappears," I said, "then you'll disappear too, Dad. You'll never have been born. And neither will I."

Dad looked startled. "You're right," he said. "I never thought of it like that."

"We have to do something fast," I said. "If not, all three of us are history."

"We won't even be history," said Dad sadly. "We'll be never-was."

Grandma reached out to Dad to comfort him. Just then something clanged on the floor. I looked down. It was Grandma's Rockettes bracelet. It had fallen off her skinny little-girl wrist. I remembered what Mrs. Coleman-Levin had said about the special powers of the bracelet. Hmmm...

I tried to ask Grandma Leah more about the bracelet and what had happened at the airport. But it was no use. She had lost another year or two. And all she cared about was her birthday.

"Tomorrow's my birthday!" Grandma Leah announced.

"That's right, dear," said Dad.

"How old will I be on my birthday?" asked Grandma Leah.

"I don't know, dear," said Dad. "How old do you think?"

"Seven!" said Grandma Leah.

"Oh, boy," I groaned.

"Or six!" said Grandma Leah. "How old am I now? Five?"

"Dad, this is getting really serious," I said. "What are we going to do?"

"I don't know," said Dad. "But we've got to do something today. Tomorrow may be too late. For all of us."

"Tomorrow's my *birthday*!" Grandma

Leah sang happily. She didn't even seem to remember how upset she was only a moment ago. Or why.

"That's right, dear," said my dad. He patted her on the head.

"I can't help thinking that bracelet of hers has something to do with all of this," I said.

"You could be right," said Dad. "That and the broken metal detector at the airport."

"Exactly," I said. "You know, Mrs. Coleman-Levin said one of the crystals in the bracelet has a strong electromagnetic field. Maybe wearing the bracelet and walking backwards through the broken metal detector was what did this. Maybe Grandma got zapped somehow and that started turning her younger."

"Stranger things have happened," said my dad. "Maybe you are right."

"If I'm right, then our only hope is to get her back in that metal detector as fast as possible. And try to reverse it."

"It's worth a try," said my dad.

"Then we'd better get to the airport now," I said. "There isn't a minute to lose."

Dad got us another cab and told the driver to go straight to LaGuardia. On the way to the airport, Grandma lost another couple of years. She was chattier than ever.

"Tomorrow my *birfday*!" she announced to the cab driver.

"That's nice, little girl," said the driver.

Grandma turned to my dad.

"Am I having a birfday party?" she asked.

"We'll see," said Dad.

"I *want* a birfday party!" she said.

"OK," said Dad. "We'll see what we can do."

"A birfday party with a *cake*," said

Grandma Leah. "And *balloons*. And a *clown*. And *presents*."

"We'll see what we can do," said Dad.

"What presents you buy me for my birfday?" asked Grandma Leah.

"I don't know," said my dad. "What would you like?"

"A pony," said Grandma Leah.

"Well, Mom," said Dad, "I'm not sure we can do that."

My grandma burst into tears.

"I wanna *pony*!" she yelled.

"But, Grandma," I said, "you live in an apartment. How can you keep a pony in an apartment?"

"A *little* pony!" she yelled. "I wanna *little* pony for my 'part-ment!"

Dad turned to me.

"What can I do here?" he asked.

"Tell her she can have a pony," said the driver.

Chapter 6

"Let me see if I've got this straight," said the head of airport security.

We were sitting in his office at La-Guardia Airport.

"You're telling me that this little girl here is eighty-nine years old," said the man.

"*Tomorrow*!" shouted Grandma Leah. "My eighty-ninth birfday's *tomorrow*! I'm getting a *pony*!"

The man frowned at my grandma on the sofa. Then he continued.

"You're telling me she keeps getting younger and younger. You're telling me that's because she went through a broken metal detector in this airport."

"Right," said my dad.

"You're telling me the only way you can save her life and yours is for her to go back through the broken metal detector. I have to crank it up and make it go backwards. Is that right? Is that what you're asking me to do?"

"You don't have to believe me," said Dad. "Just do it to humor us."

"Airport security does not do things to humor people," said the man.

"Then do it to avoid a big lawsuit," said Dad.

The head of security took us to the metal detector. It was in a storeroom at the back of the terminal.

"All right," he said. "This is the machine she went through the other day."

"The broken one?" said Dad.

"I'm not saying it's broken," said the man. "I'm not saying it's *not* broken. If we let the little girl stand under it, do you promise to go home and leave us alone?"

"We promise," said Dad.

"Fine," said the man. He had all sorts of papers for Dad to sign. I guess that was so we couldn't sue the airport later.

"OK, Grandma," I said, "go and stand in that doorway there."

"No," said my grandma.

"No?" I said. "Why not?"

"I 'fraid," said my grandma.

"Mom, there's nothing to be afraid of," said Dad.

"I 'fraid to go *alone*," said my grandma.

"OK, Grandma," I said, "take my hand. You stand in the doorway, and I'll hold your hand. And here. Hang on to your Rockettes bracelet with the other hand."

Grandma held my hand and her copper bracelet. She stood under the metal detector doorway. I stood on the other side of it.

"Now crank it up in reverse," said my dad.

"There isn't any reverse," said the man.

"Well, then, just do the opposite of what you normally do," said my dad.

The man sighed. He pushed a few switches. He turned a few knobs. I heard a slight humming sound.

Grandma stood under the metal detector, looking maybe two years old. She looked really scared. I felt sorry for her.

At first nothing happened. Then the machine started blipping and blooping and making other strange noises. There was a flash of light and a shower of sparks.

Grandma twitched. And then...she started growing!

"Stay in there, Mom! It's starting to work!" Dad shouted.

Grandma's arms grew longer. And her legs. Pretty soon she looked about five. Grandma stopped crying. She seemed a whole lot happier. The machine kept humming. Soon she was the size of an eight-year-old.

"How are you feeling now, Grandma?" I asked.

"Lots better," she said. She squeezed my hand.

Grandma Leah was growing faster and faster. Now she was a teenager. Her clothes didn't fit her any longer. Dad took his coat and wrapped it around Grandma in the doorway.

Grandma grew older. Now she was nearly

twenty. Now thirty. The machine was speed-
ing up. Now she was forty-five.

"You can stop anytime you like, Mom,"
said my dad. "Just step out from under the
doorway."

Grandma shook her head.

Grandma had hit sixty. Then seventy. She
was starting to look like her old self.

"Mom, why not stop now?" said my dad.
"You're seventy years old. That's a good age
to be."

Grandma Leah shook her head.

"I've already been seventy," she said. "It
was a fine age, but I've done that age already. I want to go back to the age I was before all of this nonsense began."

"You mean eighty-eight going on eighty-
nine?" I said.

Grandma nodded. Her hair was all gray
again. There were wrinkles in her face.

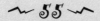

"It's the age I know best," she said. "The age I'm most comfortable with."

Now she was seventy-five. Now eighty. A few seconds later she looked exactly the way she had when she arrived in New York. She stepped out from under the metal detector.

More sparks shot out of the doorway. There was another flash. Then smoke started pouring out of it. The head of airport security grabbed a fire extinguisher and aimed it at the doorway. There was an explosion. Then everything was covered with white foam.

Chapter 7

The Rockettes reunion at Radio City Music Hall was great. Since Grandma Leah hadn't been at the rehearsal, nobody thought she'd be at the performance. Everybody was pumped to see her, and they made a big fuss over her. Grandma loved every minute of it. And we were happy that she was back to normal.

There were a lot of former Rockettes there. Although they were all younger than my grandma, most of them looked way older.

"Leah," they said, "you look so *young*. How in the world do you manage to look so young after all these years?"

Grandma Leah just smiled. Then she looked at Dad and me and smiled some more. She really did seem exactly the same as when she arrived. A little peppier, maybe.

Except there was one small thing. When we took her to the airport for her flight home, Grandma Leah stopped and bought two audio cassettes. One was the New York Philharmonic Orchestra playing Beethoven's Fifth Symphony. The other was Snoop Doggy Dogg.

NOV   2005